HERRERASAURUS

DSUNGARIPTERUS

STYGIMOLOCH

CENTROSAURUS

MONOLOPHOSAURUS

SEGNOSAURUS

IGUANODON

SILVISAURUS

DIPLODOCUS

CERATOSAURUS

P9-CSV-757

JANE YOLEN

How Do Dinosaurs

Go to School?

Illustrated by

MARK TEAGUE

THE BLUE SKY PRESS

An Imprint of Scholastic Inc. · New York

ALEXANDRIA LIBRARY
ALEXANDRIA, VA 22304

THE BLUE SKY PRESS

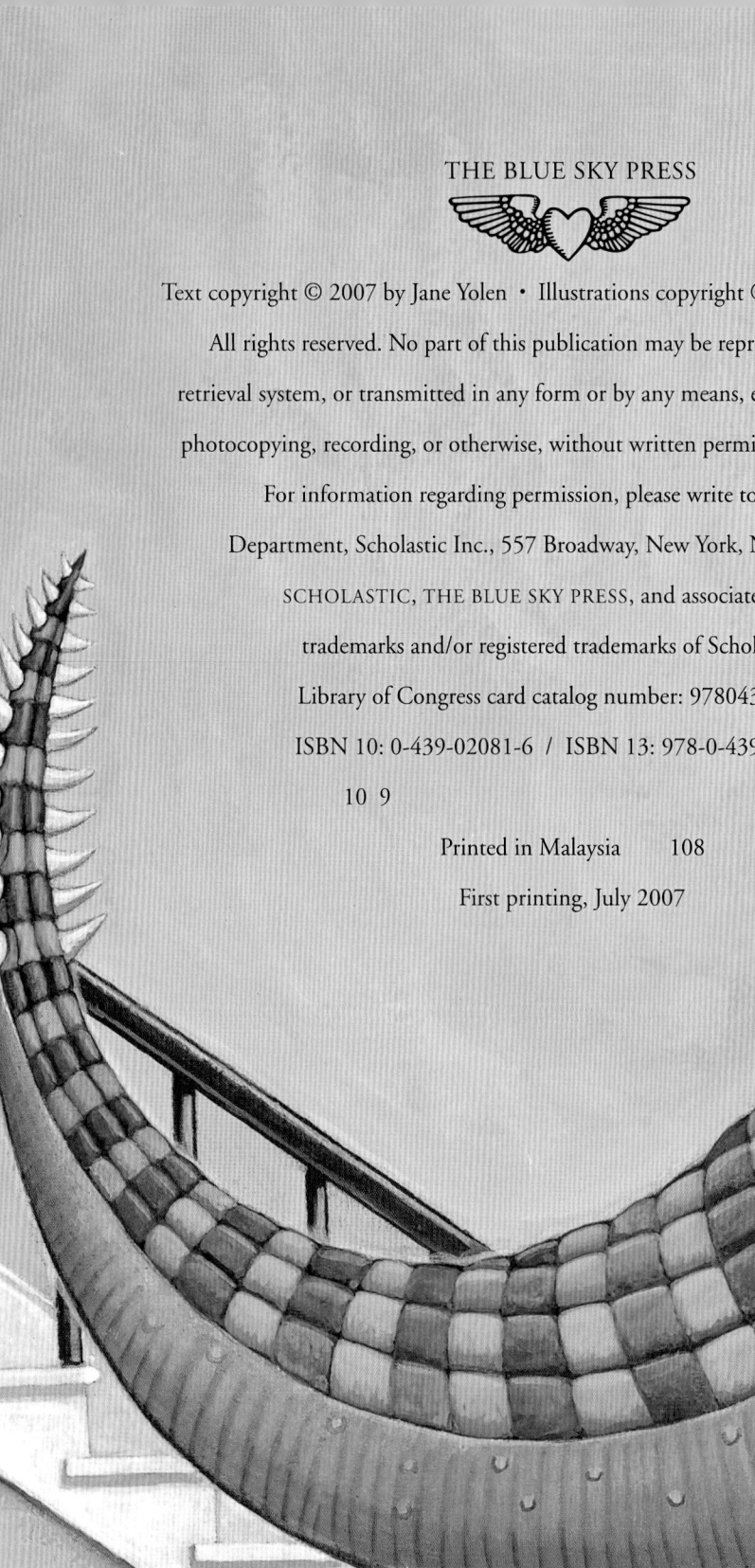

Text copyright © 2007 by Jane Yolen · Illustrations copyright © 2007 by Mark Teague

All rights reserved. No part of this publication may be reproduced, stored in a
retrieval system, or transmitted in any form or by any means, electronic, mechanical,
photocopying, recording, or otherwise, without written permission of the publisher.

For information regarding permission, please write to: Permissions
Department, Scholastic Inc., 557 Broadway, New York, New York 10012.

SCHOLASTIC, THE BLUE SKY PRESS, and associated logos are
trademarks and/or registered trademarks of Scholastic Inc.

Library of Congress card catalog number: 9780439241021

ISBN 10: 0-439-02081-6 / ISBN 13: 978-0-439-02081-7

10 9   13 14 15

Printed in Malaysia   108

First printing, July 2007

For dino-mite editor Bonnie Verburg,
who has always loved these books!
J. Y.

To Bonnie Verburg, for making great books,
and to Kathy Westray, for making them beautiful.
M. T.

How does a dinosaur

go to school?

Does he walk?

Does he ride in

a busy car pool?

CENTROSAURUS

Does he drag his long tail?

Is he late for the bus?

Does he stomp all four feet?

Does he make a big fuss?

When he gets to the school
does he roughhouse and punch?
Does he make a quick grab
for a classmate's packed lunch?

Does he race up the stairs

right ahead of the bell?

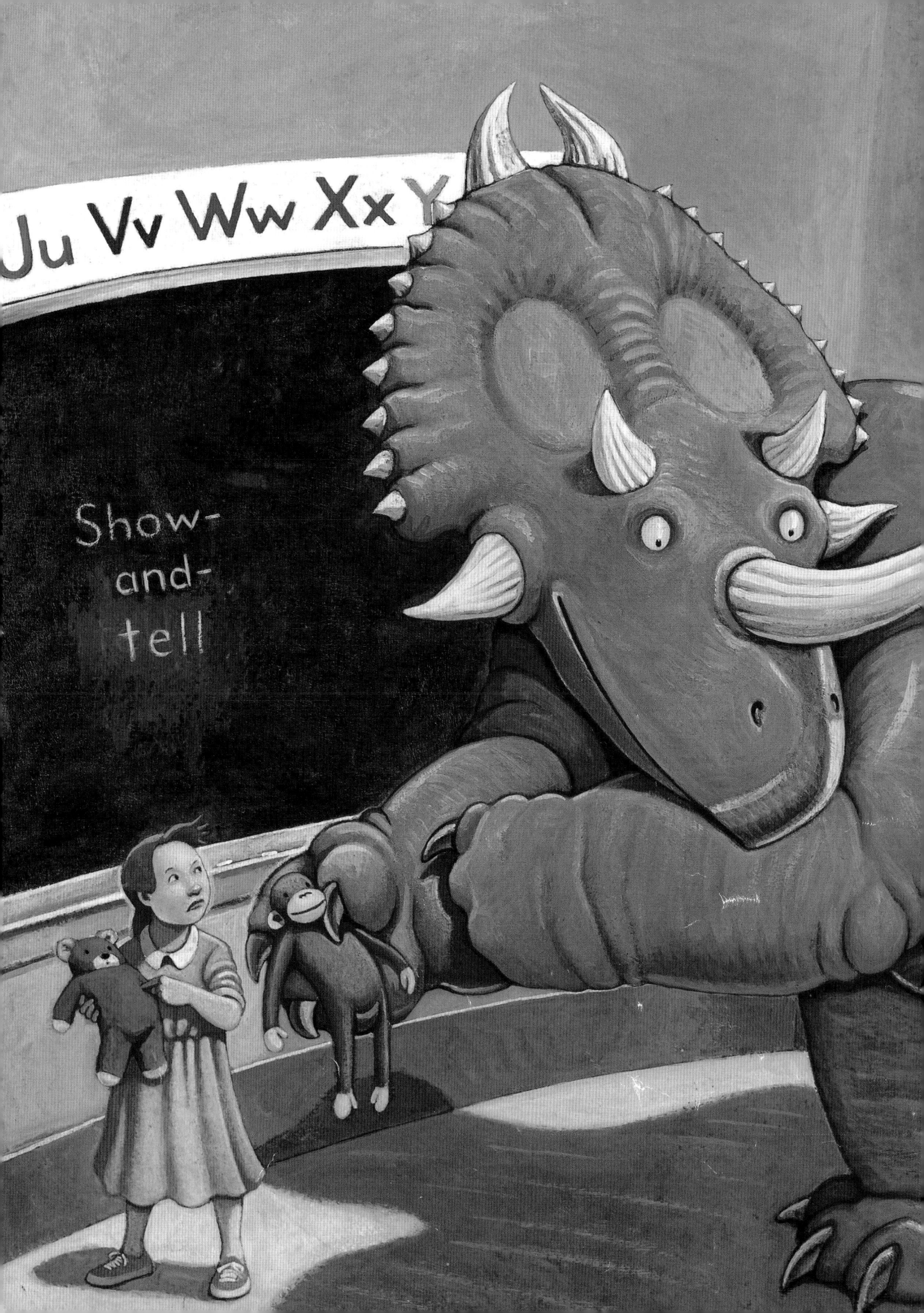

Does he interrupt class

with his own show-and-tell?

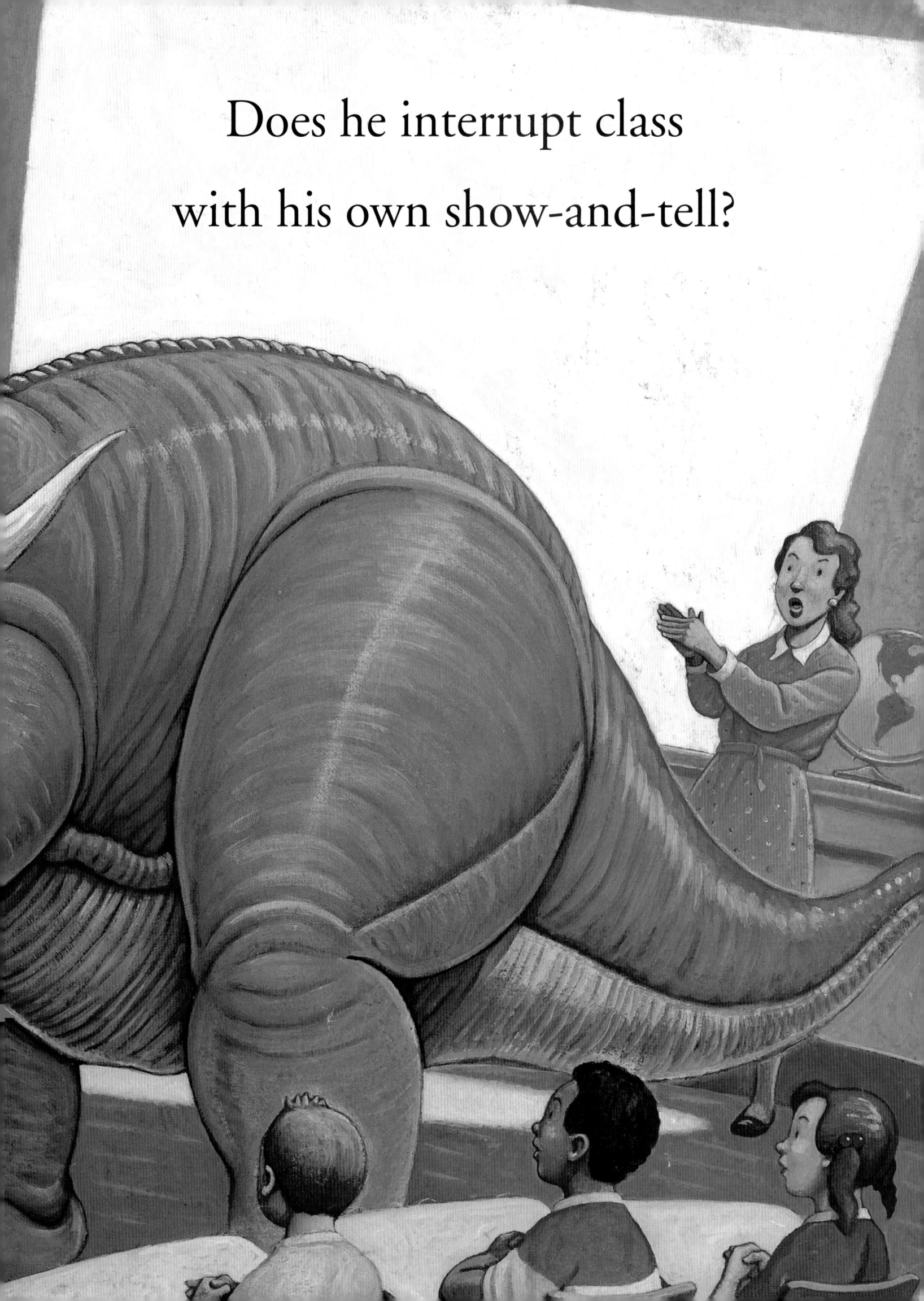

DOES A DINOSAUR YELL?

And when in the classroom,
plunked down in his chair,
does a dinosaur fidget,
his tail in the air?

Does he growl

during chalk talks,

or roar out of turn?

Does he make it too hard
for the others to learn?

Does he stir up
the classroom
by making
a noise?

Does he tease all the girls?

Does he pick on the boys?

No . . .

A dinosaur carefully
raises his hand.
He helps out his classmates
with projects
they've planned.

At recess he plays
with a number of friends,
and growls at the bullies
till bullying ends.

He tidies his desk,

then he leaps

out the door.

Good work.

Good work, little dinosaur.

HERRERASAURUS

DSUNGARIPTERUS

STYGIMOLOCH

CENTROSAURUS

MONOLOPHOSAURUS

SEGNOSAURUS

IGUANODON

SILVISAURUS

DIPLODOCUS

CERATOSAURUS

RECEIVED

JUN 24 2014

BY: